P9-CDW-633

Trixie
the Halloween
Fairy

To Susan, who always has a Halloween
trick (and treat!) up her sleeve.

Special thanks to
Kristin Earhart

If you purchased this book without a cover, you should be aware that
this book is stolen property. It was reported as "unsold and destroyed"
to the publisher, and neither the author nor the publisher has received
any payment for this "stripped book."

No part of this work may be reproduced, stored in a retrieval system,
or transmitted in any form or by any means, electronic, mechanical,
photocopying, recording, or otherwise, without written permission
of the publisher. For information regarding permission, write to
Rainbow Magic Limited, c/o HIT Entertainment, 830 South
Greenville Avenue, Allen, TX 75002-3320.

ISBN-10: 0-545-10613-3
ISBN-13: 978-0-545-10613-9

Copyright © 2009 by Rainbow Magic Limited.

All rights reserved. Published by Scholastic Inc., 557 Broadway, New
York, NY 10012, by arrangement with Rainbow Magic Limited.

SCHOLASTIC, LITTLE APPLE, and associated logos are
trademarks and/or registered trademarks of Scholastic Inc.
RAINBOW MAGIC is a trademark of Rainbow Magic Limited.
Reg. U.S. Patent & Trademark Office and other countries.
HIT and the HIT logo are trademarks of HIT Entertainment.

12 11 10 9 8 7   14/0
Printed in the U.S.A.

First printing, July 2009

Trixie
the Halloween
Fairy

by Daisy Meadows

LITTLE APPLE

SCHOLASTIC INC.

New York   Toronto   London   Auckland   Sydney
Mexico City   New Delhi   Hong Kong   Buenos Aires

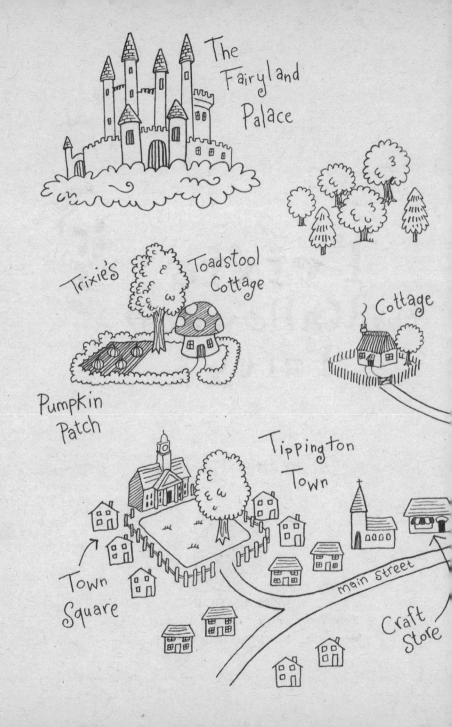

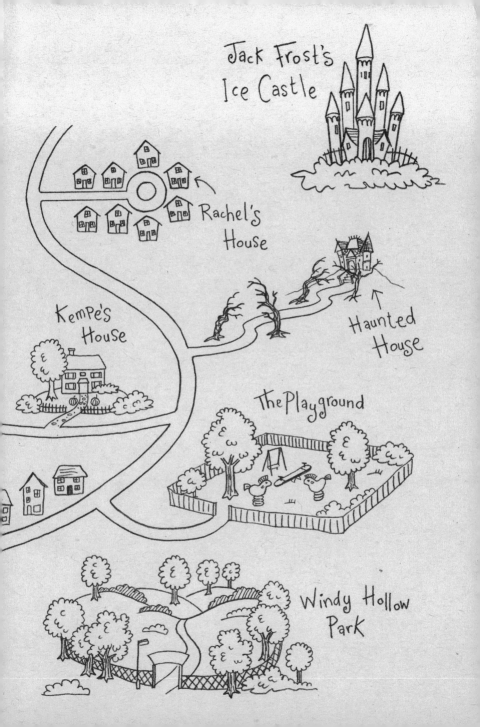

Trixie
the Halloween
Fairy

The Chocolate Bar Chase

I, Jack Frost, have planned a nasty scare.
Indeed, all humans should beware.
This year, Halloween will be all trick — no treat,
Since my goblins stole what makes the day so sweet.

To the world of humans the goblins go.
The magic candy is lost and must stay so.
All kids in costume will have a mighty fright,
When they have no fun on Halloween night.

**Find the hidden letters in the pumpkins
throughout this book. Unscramble all 12 letters to
spell a special Halloween phrase!**

Contents

Buttons Barks

"I can't wait to show you the fairy wings," Rachel Walker said to her best friend, Kirsty Tate, as they climbed the stairs to Rachel's room.

"I'm excited to see them," Kirsty replied. "It will be so much fun to trick-or-treat together!"

Kirsty was visiting Rachel while her parents were away at a wedding, and it just happened to be Halloween weekend! They were both going to dress up as fairies. The two girls exchanged smiles as Rachel lifted the lid of a storage box. Inside were two sets of glittery fairy wings: one in a pale pink and the other in a light purple.

"Oh, Rachel! They look almost real," Kirsty said, giving her friend a knowing look. After all, the girls knew just how real fairies' wings looked. They were friends with the fairies!

Rachel and Kirsty met during vacation with their families on beautiful Rainspell Island. There, they helped the Rainbow Fairies get back to Fairyland after they had been banished by the wicked Jack Frost. Since then, the girls had helped lots of fairies. Now the king and queen of Fairyland looked to them whenever Jack Frost was up to his old tricks.

"I'm going to try mine on," Kirsty said, carefully lifting up a sparkly set of wings.

Just then, they heard a loud bark. Buttons, Rachel's adorable sheepdog, raced into the room. He knocked into Kirsty and tore through the storage bin on his way to the window.

"Buttons!" Rachel yelled as the

costumes flew up in the
air. Buttons kept
barking at
something outside.
Then he turned to
Rachel and whimpered.
"What is it, boy?"
Rachel asked with
concern.

"Oh! There's a kitten in the tree!"
Kirsty said, pointing out the window.
The kitten was black from its nose to
its tail.

"That's strange," Rachel said. "Buttons
usually loves cats."

Now the big sheepdog pawed at the
window.

"Do you think the kitten's stuck?"
Kirsty asked. "Maybe it needs our help."

But at that moment, the little black cat
leaped onto a nearby branch. It strutted
past the window and seemed to look
right at Buttons and the girls, then
scurried down another tree.

Buttons let out a yelp, dashed from the
room, and ran down the stairs.

"Weird," Rachel said with a laugh.

Kirsty nodded before letting out a
groan. "Oh no! Look at
our costumes!"

Rachel bent down and
lifted up her wings. The
thin fabric had a big tear
in it. Kirsty's wings
looked the same. "It
must have happened
when Buttons

raced through here. His nails are
so sharp!"

"But that's not all that's wrong,"
Kirsty said, glancing around. "The
glitter seems to have fallen off the fabric.
The wings aren't shimmery anymore.
And it looks like one of our wands
is missing."

"I don't see my fun fairy tights, either," Rachel confessed, looking around the room and under her bed. She sat up and sighed.

"I think there may be something mysterious going on here," Kirsty said.

"Mysterious, or magical?" Rachel whispered.

Kirsty's eyes sparkled. She hoped her friend was right! "Either way, I guess we'll have to start over with our fairy costumes."

"Let's go to the costume and craft shop
to pick up some supplies," Rachel
suggested. "We only have two days left
until Halloween!"

Costume Chaos

Rachel and Kirsty made a list of what they needed at the costume shop and grabbed their bags. Then Rachel told her mom where they were going.

As they walked down the street, the girls wondered what had happened to the other parts of their costumes. "It doesn't make sense," Kirsty said. "I remember seeing two wands in the box."

Rachel shrugged her shoulders. "I don't know, either," she said. "But I'm sure we'll find everything we need at

Costumes, Cauldrons, and Crafts. It's the best Halloween store. I know the owner, Mrs. Burns. She has all kinds of fairy stuff."

The girls walked toward the center of town. The sun was out, and the air was cool and crisp. "It feels like it's almost Halloween," Kirsty said, pulling a scarf from her pocket. "And, look! That looks just like a haunted house!"

Rachel knew exactly which house her friend meant. It was a three-story Victorian mansion with a big porch and lots of windows. The house sat at the end of a long driveway that was lined with crooked trees. "Don't worry," Rachel assured Kirsty. "It's just an old house that nobody has lived in for years. There are stories that it's haunted, but they aren't true."

Just then, Rachel looked
at the third-floor
window and thought
she saw someone
there. "Kirsty!" she
exclaimed, but the
figure disappeared before
she could say more. "Oh, never
mind." Rachel tried to pretend that she'd
made a mistake, but she didn't think
she had imagined it.

When they came to the town
square, the girls noticed lots of other
people heading for the costume shop. "It's
always busy this time of year," Rachel
explained, pulling the door open.

But she gasped when she looked
around the crowded store. Parents and
kids were everywhere, and they all

looked upset. There was a long line
behind a sign that read RETURNS.
Two grumpy mothers in the line were
peering into their bags. "My son's
astronaut costume has bunny ears instead
of an oxygen helmet," one complained,
shaking her head.

"I bought a ballerina outfit, but it has

fireman boots instead of ballet
shoes," the other responded.

"All of those people bought
costumes that are mixed up?"
Kirsty whispered in disbelief.

"I guess so," Rachel
responded. "There's Mrs.
Burns," she said, pointing to a woman

carrying a straw basket,
but the storeowner
didn't notice the girls.
She was too busy
rushing around,
clicking her tongue
with concern as she
looked at the
jumbled shelves.

As the friends
walked toward
the back of the
store, all the
customers were
grumbling. No one
could find anything.
The girls passed a
group of boys who were
digging through a bin of hats

and wigs, trying things on and throwing them to the air with loud grunts. *No wonder the store is such a mess*, Kirsty thought. Just then, Rachel stopped. "This is where the fairy stuff always is," she said, pointing to a nearby shelf, "but it's not here now." "And what *is* here is all mixed up," Kirsty noted as she looked at a parrot mask with a long, gray trunk instead of a beak.

Next, she picked up a pretty, purple, cone-shaped princess hat. But instead of having ribbons flowing from the pointy top, there were rubber snakes with wagging red tongues.

"Yuck," Rachel declared.

"You can say that again," a twinkling voice sang out.

With that, a burst of
star-shaped sparkles
filled the air, and a
tiny fairy flew out
from behind the
princess hat. The fairy
wore a short and
swingy orange dress
with a silky black
sash, and black-and-
orange striped tights. A
star pendant hung around
her neck, and she had a mischievous grin.

"You must be Rachel and Kirsty," the
fairy said. "I'm Trixie, the one and only
Halloween Fairy. I need your help!"

Three Treats

Rachel and Kirsty gasped in surprise. They couldn't take their eyes off the tiny fairy's glittery wings, which were especially sparkly in the dim store.

"It's nice to meet you," Rachel and Kirsty said at once. They loved meeting new fairies!

"And it's a pleasure meeting you, too. You're quite famous in Fairyland," Trixie said.

The girls smiled at each other. "Trixie, what's wrong?" Kirsty asked, her smile fading. "Why do you need our help?"

"Oh!" Trixie sighed. Her clever smirk quickly fell into a frown. "Halloween is in terrible trouble."

"What happened?" Rachel questioned.

Trixie sighed. "It all started yesterday," the fairy began. "I had just finished making my magic Halloween candy.

Every year, I make three kinds of candy: chocolate bars, candy corn, and caramel apples." The fairy paused and licked her lips. "Oh, where was I?" she asked herself. "Ah, yes. I  sprinkle one piece of candy from each batch with my special star-shaped fairy dust. These three enchanted pieces of candy hold the Halloween magic! Without them, Halloween wouldn't be the same."

"Did something happen to the candy?" Kirsty asked, biting her fingernail.

"It's missing!" Trixie cried. Kirsty and Rachel listened closely. Trixie told them that each piece of candy had an important job: The chocolate bar helped make sure everyone had a costume and looked good. The magic candy corn's job was to make sure there was plenty of candy and that it tasted extra sweet.

Finally, the caramel apple helped boost the Halloween spirit — it let everyone enjoy the magic of the holiday.

"I wrap each magic piece of candy in an orange glitter wrapper," Trixie added with a twinkle in her eye. "The king and queen give them away as prizes at our Halloween Ball."

"Wow. I didn't even know you celebrated Halloween in Fairyland," Kirsty said.

"Oh yes," Trixie replied. "We love Halloween. It's one of the few days that people in the human world believe in the magic that lives in Fairyland all year long." Then Trixie scowled a little. "Except Jack Frost. He doesn't want humans to have all of the fun. This year, he came up with a nasty plan."

Trixie explained that she was watering her pumpkin patch when she heard a big racket.

"Oh no," Kirsty said, biting her lip.

"You guessed it," said Trixie, putting her hands on her hips. The fairy's eyes

were serious as she told them about Jack
Frost's goblins, who had snuck into her
toadstool cottage to steal the magic
candies. "They were almost to the edge
of the Fairyland Forest when I spotted
them: seven green goblins with chocolate
smeared on their hands and faces. Just as
I lifted my wand to stop them, Jack Frost

appeared. The icy lightning bolts from his wand crashed into my star sparkles, and the goblins disappeared in a cloudy haze. My magic candy was gone, too!"

"Oh no! We have to get it back!" Rachel cried. She couldn't imagine Halloween without costumes, candy, and lots of fun.

"Thank you!" Trixie said with a grateful smile. "But there's just one more thing." The fairy's deep brown eyes grew wide. "We can't let the candy fall into the wrong hands. If someone who doesn't

believe in Halloween eats a piece, that
part of Halloween will be ruined."

Rachel and Kirsty gulped.

Just then, one of the noisy boys who
had been rummaging through the hat
bins stamped his feet. "It's not here!" he
whined. "I'm looking somewhere else."
The others followed, all wearing a hat or
piece of shiny jewelry.

"Did you see that?" Kirsty asked.

"It's awful," Trixie said, shaking her head. "Those boys don't have any real Halloween spirit."

"And they didn't have any shoes!" Rachel blurted out. "But they did have big, green feet."

"Exactly," Kirsty agreed. "Trixie, I think we've found the goblins!"

Goblins on the Go

Kirsty, Rachel, and Trixie rushed after the goblins.

"They went in there!" Rachel said, pointing at a heavy door with a sign that read STORAGE ROOM.

"Then we have to go in there, too," Trixie announced. She pointed her wand,

and the door opened with a burst of star sparkles. "Trixie!" Kirsty gasped. "You have to be more careful. Someone might see you!"

Trixie quickly flew into Kirsty's pocket until they were safe inside the storage room, which was almost as big as the store itself. There was row after row of shelves, each piled high with boxes — but no sign of goblins.

"Mrs. Burns always has a basket of candy on the counter," Rachel whispered. "Maybe she keeps her candy in here."

"And maybe the glitter chocolate bar is with it!" Trixie declared.

The girls had to tiptoe around open costume boxes that littered the floor. "This room is as messy as the store," Kirsty commented.

"It's because the glitter chocolate bar is missing," Trixie explained. "Everything that has do with costumes is all mixed up." E

"That's what happened to our wings!"
Rachel said.

"And the other wand," Kirsty added.

Realizing it was safe, Trixie zoomed
out of Kirsty's pocket. "Let's go find
those goblins and my candy!" she
declared.

The girls raced after the fairy, dodging
piles of costumes and crafts as they went.

When they saw
blasts of icy sparks
in the next aisle,
they slowed down
and peeked around
the corner.
"Jack Frost gave
them a wand,"
Trixie said. "You have to be careful. It
can mix up anything!"

A goblin with extra pointy ears held the wand. He aimed it at a tall goblin dressed as a policeman. "I want to be the policeman!" he yelled, but the goblin in the policeman costume just shook his head. Just then, icy bolts shot from the goblin's wand, and the policeman's blue

uniform shirt changed to a sparkly yellow halter top.

"Change it back!" yelped the tall goblin, blowing on his police whistle.

"Uh-unh." The pointy-eared goblin refused, then aimed the wand again and turned a ferocious dragon costume bright pink with purple flowers.

"That explains the mismatched costumes," Kirsty whispered.

The other goblins were pushing down boxes and ripping through them.

"They must think one of the magic candies is here," Trixie guessed.

At that moment, Kirsty thought she saw a flash of something orange and glittery. "They found a piece of candy!" Kirsty yelled, not able to control her excitement. "It must be the chocolate bar. Let's get it!"

As soon as the goblins heard Kirsty, they stopped what they were doing and raced toward the back door.

Hot on the goblins' trail, the girls ran through the door and into the alley with

Trixie flying overhead. As they chased
the goblins around the corner, they
searched for another glimpse of the glitter
wrapper. The seven goblins were running
in a mob, dropping wigs and hats
wherever they went.

"Oh no! They're headed for the town square," Rachel said as the goblins made their way across Main Street and onto the grassy area in the center of the village. Trixie and the girls looked around frantically. They couldn't let

anyone else spot the goblins! The three friends were gaining on the goblin gang, but they still had no idea which one had the magic candy.

All at once, a black cat sprung out of a tree and pounced down in the middle of the goblins' path.

"Yikes!" screeched the first goblin, as he tripped and fell. When he tried to get up, another goblin toppled over him, then another, until they were all in a giant heap.

"It's the little black cat!" Rachel said, watching the kitten climb from the bottom of the goblin pile. It seemed to look at the girls and Trixie before bounding across the village green and out of sight. "And here's our orange glitter," said Kirsty. She sounded disappointed as she picked up something from the ground. "It isn't a magic candy wrapper at all." The orange glitter was on a

tiger mask that a
goblin had taken
from the storage
room. "Now we
have to start
all over."

"Don't worry,
Trixie, we'll find
the magic candies,"
Rachel said, but
when she looked around,
she didn't see Trixie anywhere.

Where had their fairy friend gone?

Lost and Found

The girls quickly walked away from the
goblins, who were still in a jumble, and
started searching for Trixie. At once, the
fairy zipped down from high in the sky.

"Did you find something?" Rachel
asked hopefully.

"Not really," Trixie responded. "I was
looking for Moonlight."

"Moonlight?" Kirsty questioned, shielding her eyes as she glanced up at the sunny sky.

"The little black kitten," Trixie replied with a small smile. "He must have gotten mixed up in the spells that sent the magic candy into the human world."

"Is he your kitten?" Rachel asked.

"Not really. He's been hanging around my cottage in Fairyland ever since I started making my Halloween candy," the fairy explained. "He's kind of shy,

very spunky, and he seems to have a
sweet tooth."

"We saw him this morning, too,"
Kirsty said. "At Rachel's house."

"I hope he doesn't get hurt
here. I'm sure the king and
queen would want me to
get him back to
Fairyland, but we
have to find the
magic candy first,"
Trixie said.

Kirsty and Rachel knew they only
had two days until Halloween, and they
still needed to find all three pieces of
magical candy!

The three friends headed back to the
costume shop. Along the way, they

picked up the costumes that the goblins had dropped in their mad dash from the storage room.

"If the orange glitter were really just a tiger mask, the magic chocolate bar could still be at Costumes, Caldrons, and Crafts," Kirsty said.

"Or somewhere else," Rachel admitted.

"We should trust that the magic will come to us," Trixie reminded them. The queen of Fairyland often gave the girls that same advice!

When they arrived back at the store, Mrs. Burns was trying to clean up the mess. "I just don't understand what happened," she said. "I don't like it when people are unhappy with their costumes. I can't even find the candy that I had to give away. It doesn't feel like Halloween at all!"

Still, the storeowner smiled when she saw Rachel. As soon as she heard that Rachel and Kirsty needed fairy supplies for their costumes, she hurried off to find wings and other things.

"Let's help pick up," Rachel suggested.

Kirsty, Rachel, and Trixie went
to the back of the store and
started to put things back
in the right place.
When no one was
looking, Trixie
used her wand to
send sticks of
makeup and
trick-or-treat
bags back to the
shelves with a
sparkle. In no
time, the floors
were clean and the
bins were almost full.

"If we don't find new
wings, I could always be
a clown," Rachel said with a

laugh as she picked up a bright red clown wig. As she plopped it on her head, candy came showering down out of the wig and landed in a heap on the floor. "Look!" Kirsty exclaimed, pointing to a glittery orange wrapper at the very top of the pile. "Oh, Rachel," Mrs. Burns said, rushing forward. "You found our trick-or-treat candy! And I just happen to have the basket right here!"

Kirsty held her breath as the storeowner bent down to gather the candy. Immediately, the girls kneeled down to help. Rachel gave Kirsty a concerned glance as they watched Mrs. Burns toss the glitter chocolate into the straw basket.

"It just hasn't felt like Halloween without our candy basket," Mrs. Burns said, standing up and starting to walk away. Kirsty's face dropped as the woman went around the corner.

"What am I thinking?" Mrs. Burns asked, hurrying back. "Would you like a piece?"

As soon as Mrs. Burns made the offer, Kirsty's hand sprang forward to grab the

chocolate bar with the orange
glitter wrapper. "Thank you,
Mrs. Burns," she said,
beaming. "It does feel more
like Halloween already."
Kirsty secretly held the
candy behind her back,
and Trixie swooped
down to pick it up.

"And look!" Mrs. Burns
declared, pointing to something on the
very top shelf. "I see my favorite fairy
wings. I had wondered where they were
hiding." The storeowner climbed up the
old, rolling ladder to pull the sparkly
packages off the shelf. She handed one to
Rachel and another to Kirsty. "You girls
have been such a help. Please take these
as a special thank you."

"Oh, Mrs. Burns, they're beautiful,"
Rachel said with a delighted sigh.

"Thank you so much," added Kirsty.

As the girls grinned, they saw Trixie
swoosh into the air behind Mrs. Burns.
The cheery fairy spun around and gave
the glittery orange candy a little kiss.
Rachel and Kirsty watched her fly away,

knowing she was
headed back to
Fairyland.

"Our costumes are
going to look
amazing," Rachel
said, turning to Kirsty.

"And once Trixie
returns the chocolate candy to
Fairyland, everyone's costumes will start
to come together," agreed Kirsty. "Now
we just have two more
pieces of candy to track
down, and we'll all
have a happy
Halloween!"

The Candy
Corn Caper

Contents

All Dressed Up

"Happy Halloween!" Mr. Walker said, snapping a picture of Rachel and Kirsty with his camera. "You look great!"

"Just like real fairies," Rachel's mom added, her hands clasped.

Rachel and Kirsty smiled at each other. They both wore beautiful, glittery wings on their backs. Kirsty had on a short,

purple, pleated skirt and a lilac wrap
sweater with bell sleeves. Rachel had
chosen a pretty green sweater dress with
ballerina flats. A silver locket shimmered
around each of their necks. The lockets
had been gifts from the king and queen
of Fairyland.

"I wonder where our newest fairy
friend could be," Kirsty whispered,

suddenly concerned. The
best friends had not seen
Trixie since they had
found the magic
chocolate bar in the
costume shop a few days
earlier.

Ding-dong! Ding-dong!

"I'll get that," Mr. Walker
offered. He put on a cowboy
hat to match his jeans and boots as he
headed to the front hall. Rachel's mom
followed him. She wore a matching hat
with a long jean skirt. Her checked shirt
was tied at the waist.

"We know Trixie made it to Fairyland
with the chocolate bar," Rachel said
under her breath. "All of our costumes

look amazing! If the chocolate wasn't back in Fairyland, the costumes would still be mixed up."

"Trixie will show up soon," Kirsty said with a sigh. "I'm sure of it." It was almost time to trick-or-treat, and they still had to find two more pieces of glitter candy!

Just then, Rachel's dad rushed into the living room. "Girls, do you know where our candy went? It seems to have disappeared. Even the bowl is gone!"

Kirsty and Rachel looked at each other.

"We have no idea where it is," Rachel replied. It was true. They didn't have any idea where the candy was, but they did have an idea of *why* it was missing. It was all because of Jack Frost and his tricky goblins!

"Well, there are a bunch of ghosts at our door, and we don't have anything to give them." Mr. Walker rushed to the kitchen, his boots clip-clopping on the floor.

Buttons let out a bark. "Oh, I forgot how nervous Buttons gets on Halloween," Rachel said, running toward the front door. She got there just in time to grab the wooly sheepdog's collar. "It's okay, boy. He doesn't like all of the costumes," Rachel explained.

The girls looked out the open door into the dusky night. The neighborhood was starting to fill with firemen and superheroes, princesses and knights, dinosaurs and lions.

They could see a whole band of boys dressed as ghosts scampering down the street.

"Those ghosts didn't even wait for Dad to find the candy," said Rachel.

"And look! There's Trixie's kitten, Moonlight. He's running after the ghosts," Kirsty added with a laugh. The tiny cat was leaping through the tall grass. Kirsty lowered her voice to a whisper. "I wonder if those ghosts are actually . . . goblins?"

Rachel gasped, her eyes widening.

Just then, Rachel's parents returned to the front hall. Mr. Walker was rubbing his chin. "I guess I'll have to get more candy at the store," he said. "It isn't Halloween without trick-or-treating."

"You two should get going and have fun," suggested Mrs. Walker.

The two best friends grabbed their

candy bags and straightened their wings. Kirsty waved as she headed out the door.

"We'll see you at the town party later," Rachel said, giving each of her parents a quick hug.

"Yes, you girls are going to have a busy night!" Mr. Walker replied.

Rachel and Kirsty gave each other worried looks. Little did he know. They still needed to find two more pieces of magic candy — and they were running out of time!

All Trick, No Treat

As Kirsty and Rachel headed out to the
sidewalk, they saw some older boys
stride by.

"Hey! There's a rock in this candy
wrapper!" an alien shouted to his friends.

"Yuck! In mine, too!" a football player
sputtered, wiping his mouth on his sleeve.

He threw the rock to the ground. "That was a mean trick."

Rachel shook her head and sighed, watching the boys wander away. "I guess we should trick-or-treat," she said, "and see what happens."

"Good idea," agreed Kirsty as they walked up a pebble path. The path led to a house with lot of jack-o'-lanterns placed on the steps.

Golden lights flickered through their carved faces with a spooky glow. "The Kempes live here," Rachel said. "They're friends with my parents. They always have really good candy." "I hope *they* can find their candy bowl," Kirsty said, raising her eyebrows. "Trick or treat!" the girls declared when the door opened. A woman wearing a crown smiled at them. "Just look at you," Mrs. Kempe said.

Then she paused and called over her shoulder. "Sal, come see the fairies!"

A tall man with thick, white hair appeared behind Mrs. Kempe. "Are those real wings?" he teased. "You look like you could fly away." Then he held out a basket full of candy for the girls.

Rachel and Kirsty looked at each other with surprise. The Kempes had candy

after all! There were little round peanut
butter cups, square fruit chews, and rolls
of Sweet Tarts — nothing in the shape
of rocks.

"Thank you, Mr. and Mrs. Kempe!"
Rachel exclaimed, selecting a peanut
butter cup. Kirsty took a package of
fruit chews.

"Of course," Mrs. Kempe said, waving
good-bye. "Now run along and be safe.
Happy Halloween!"

"You were right!" Kirsty cried as the
girls headed down the stairs. "They did
have great stuff! I love fruit chews."
Kirsty ripped open the paper wrapper
and popped the red candy into her mouth.
At once, her smile dropped and her nose
scrunched up. "Rachel," she said, "it
doesn't taste good." She paused, moving

the candy around in her mouth. "It doesn't taste like anything at all."

Rachel, who had just taken a nibble of her peanut butter cup, also frowned.

"I know. It's awful!" The girls immediately looked around, recognizing the voice that echoed through the air. Trixie!

The tiny fairy fluttered into view with a cloud of star-shaped fairy dust trailing behind her. The dust sparkled against the dark night sky. "It's because

the magic candy corn is still missing," Trixie explained. "The candy corn not only makes sure there is plenty of candy, but it also makes it nice and sweet. We have to find it!"

"Oh, Trixie!" Kirsty cried. "We're so glad to see you!"

"And I'm glad to see you," Trixie replied. "But there's no time to chit-chat. I think I know where the magic candy corn might be!" With that, the little Halloween fairy whizzed down the street.

A Candy Clue

Rachel and Kirsty took off, running as fast as they could. They couldn't quite keep up with Trixie. The fairy was dodging trick-or-treaters as she zoomed ahead.

"Someone's going to see her if she's not careful," Rachel said, gasping for breath.

"And she's got to slow down," Kirsty puffed. Just then, Trixie stopped in midair and looked back at the girls. "This is it!" she called, pointing to a cottage with a stone chimney and thatched roof. There was a single candle in the window, and Kirsty could just make out a broom propped up on the porch.

"Come on," Trixie said, grinning and zooming up to the door.

The cottage looked mysterious in the moonlight, but the girls felt safe with Trixie nearby. They climbed up the creaky old porch stairs.

Trixie raised her wand, and a stream of fairy dust pushed the doorbell.

"Trixie, you have to hide!" Rachel insisted, holding open her cloth candy bag. The fairy ducked inside just as the heavy wooden door swung open.

"Trick or treat!" the girls shouted.

A pale face appeared around the edge of the door. The lady had straight black hair and wore a witch's costume. "Of course," she said. "Come pick some candy out of my cauldron."

The girls peeked inside the tidy little cottage and saw a gigantic black pot right next to the door. It was empty.

"Oh no!" the lady exclaimed when she

realized the candy was gone. "You're only my second group of trick-or-treaters. I wonder if those rude little ghosts took it all." She bent over and swept her hand through the big iron pot, just to be sure that there was nothing inside. "Even the candy in the pretty glitter wrapper is gone!"

Rachel and Kirsty exchanged glances.

"There were ghosts
here before us?"
Rachel asked.

"Yes, about six or
seven of them. They
just left," the lady said,
taking off her tall,
pointy hat and looking terribly sad.
"This is the first Halloween I've had in
my own house," she added. "I wanted it
to be fun."

Kirsty felt awful for her. "We know
those ghosts," Kirsty said. "If they took
your candy, we'll get it back. Come on,
Rachel." Kirsty gave the lady a small
smile and a nod. Without another word,
she marched down the stairs.

"We're going to find the glitter candy
corn," Trixie said, fluttering out of

Rachel's cloth bag as soon as the girls were out of sight of the cottage. "If that lady is right, the ghosts must have it!"

"So all we have to do is find the ghosts — I mean, goblins," Kirsty replied. "And then all the candy will be back where it belongs."

"Okay," Rachel agreed. "Where do we start? It's getting dark, so it will be harder to find them. And we don't even know which way they went."

"First of all, I can make your wands a little more useful," Trixie responded. The fairy waved her own wand, and fairy dust swirled around the wands in Kirsty's and Rachel's hands. The

wands began to glow with a bright,
silvery light. "And it would help if those
wings really worked." With another twirl
of Trixie's wand, the girls' wings began
to sparkle. As the friends floated up into
the air, they shrank down to fairy size.

"That's much better, isn't it?" Trixie
declared, with her hands on her hips.
"Now let's go get those goblins!"

Playground Ghosts

The three fairy friends fluttered their
wings until they were high above the
trees. "We'll be able to spot that band
of ghosts much better from up here,"
Trixie said.

Kirsty and Rachel flew close behind
Trixie. They held their wands in front of
them to light the way. They were getting

closer to town, and there were more people on the sidewalks and in the streets.

"Hey, look! " Kirsty exclaimed. "I see a bunch of ghosts down there." A streetlight cast a dim glow over the nearby playground. Rachel could just make out a cluster of ghosts hidden in the shadow of a tall tree.

"They have a bunch of baskets of candy!" Trixie declared. "The magic candy corn might be there."

In the cool night, the goblins' voices carried through the air. They were grunting and grumbling as they threw candy and wrappers all around.

Kirsty gasped. "Oh no! They're eating it!" she cried. She remembered that if someone who didn't believe in Halloween ate the magic candy, then that part of Halloween would be ruined. What if the goblins ate the magic candy corn? Kirsty shivered. She couldn't bear

to think about Halloween
without the taste of rich
chocolate, or tangy
gumdrops, or spicy red
hots! "We have to do
something, and fast!"
she insisted.
"Trixie, can you turn
us into girls again?"
Rachel asked, flying lower in the sky.
"We'll have a better chance of catching
the goblins on the ground."

"Of course," Trixie said. "But I won't
change your wands. You might need the
light!"

As soon as Kirsty and Rachel were
ready, Trixie waved her wand. The
girls took off running toward the goblins
the moment their feet touched the grass.

"Stop!" they yelled at the same time.

The goblins stopped eating and tried to look around, but they couldn't see through the tiny eyeholes in their white sheets.

"Who was that?" a goblin asked, his voice muffled by the sheet over his head.

"Who cares?" another replied. "Focus! We have to find that magic candy and take it to Jack Frost."

Then a goblin peeked out from under his costume. "Oh no! It's those annoying girls again!" he yelped. "Let's get out of

here!" The goblins scrambled to throw all of the candy back into the baskets and bowls and bags. Then they stacked them up and tried to balance the towers of treats as they ran toward the street.

"They must have stolen candy from almost every house!" Kirsty said, chasing a goblin with six bowls teetering in his hands.

The goblins stumbled across
the playground, barely able
to see. One goblin ran right
up one side of a seesaw and
down the other. Another got
caught on the tire swing. But
before the girls knew it, the
goblins disappeared into the street — and
into the middle of the costume parade!

Moonlight's Magic

The street was full of people in costume.
Kirsty watched as angels and race car
drivers and bunnies marched by. Then,
out of the corner of her eye, Kirsty
glimpsed a flash of white. A ghost!

She reached out to grab the ghost's
trick-or-treat bag, but then she realized
the ghost wore tiny white sneakers.

A goblin could never fit his huge feet into those little shoes, she thought. Just as she had given up hope, Kirsty felt a tap on her shoulder.

"Look over there," said Rachel, pointing. Kirsty followed her friend's gaze and saw Trixie perched in a tree on the other side of the street. The fairy was waving her arms, and jumping up and down. "Let's go see what she wants —

before anyone else spots her!" Rachel said, grabbing Kirsty's hand and leading her through the crowd of people.

"I'm glad you saw me," Trixie said as she flew down from the tree and landed on Rachel's shoulder, "because I spotted the goblins! They went into that park!"

Rachel and Kirsty peered into the nearby dark park. "That's Windy Hollow," Rachel said with a shiver. "It won't be easy to find them in there."

"Well, let's give it our best shot," Trixie replied with a bright smile, flying into the dark night. The two friends slipped through the park gate and into the shadows after her. At once, they could hear the wind that gave the park its name. It rustled through the leaves and put a chill in the air.

"It really feels like Halloween now," Kirsty whispered as she searched the inky night for signs of goblins. There were no streetlamps, and heavy clouds covered the moon. The only light came from their three fairy wands. The girls tiptoed along, stopping every few steps to try and listen for the goblins.

"*Shhhh*," Trixie warned them. "I think we're close." The little fairy peeked over the crest of a hill and motioned for Kirsty and Rachel to stop. "They're down there," she whispered. The girls got on their hands and knees, and crawled up the grassy slope to look over the hill. Sure

enough, the group of ghosts was in the valley, rooting through the candy stash again. "If they have the magic candy corn, they're bound to find it soon," Rachel said, worried.

"Not if we find it first," Kirsty replied. "Trixie, how do you feel about playing a little Halloween trick?" Kirsty's eyes brightened as she told Rachel and Trixie her plan.

"It's worth a try," Trixie said with a smirk. "I can't do much while the candy

is missing, but I still have
enough magic for a little
trick!" She gave her
wand a twirl and recited
a spell:

The goblins think they're in disguise,
but now real ghosts are on the rise.
Raise those sheets up in the air.
Then all goblins should beware!

As soon as Trixie was done speaking,
the sheets that covered the goblins lifted
into the air. They floated just above the
goblins' heads and looked like real
ghosts!

Rachel and Kirsty gave each other a
thumbs-up and then spoke in their

spookiest voices. "*Oooooooo*,"
they moaned. "Give back
the candy you stole.
Oooooooooooo!"

At once, the
goblins looked up
and saw the sheets
fluttering the wind.

"Ghosts!" they
screeched.

"*Oooooooo*! Give
back the candy,"
the girls repeated.
The three friends
giggled. The goblins
were cowering below
the ghostly sheets,
shaking with fear.

Just then, a single

goblin yelled, "I found the magic candy corn!" He held his hand up in the air. "Hooray!"

Kirsty, Rachel, and Trixie exchanged worried glances. "What do we do now?" Kirsty whispered. "Chase him!" Rachel said. But before the friends could get to their feet, they heard a loud yowl. They saw Moonlight, the mischievous kitten, pounce onto the goblin's back. "*Ouch!*" the goblin yelped, trying to swat

Moonlight off. The other goblins
scattered in different directions until only
the one remained. All at once, Moonlight
jumped to the ground, and the last goblin
darted away after his friends.

Moonlight looked right up at Trixie
and the two girls. "Meow," the black
kitten mewed softly. "Meow, meow,
meow," he repeated before leaping into
the shadows.

"It's the glitter candy!" Trixie
exclaimed. "Moonlight is telling us that
the goblin dropped it!" The three friends

raced down the hill to where the kitten had been. Sure enough, there was the magical candy corn on the ground, along with all of the other stolen treats.

"I can't wait to get this back to Fairyland," Trixie declared, lifting the candy corn up in the air. As soon as she touched it, it shrank to its original

Fairyland size. "Then there will be candy for everyone!"

"And all of the candy will taste extra sweet," Kirsty added.

The clouds floated away and the moon brightened the night with a silvery light.

"We sure are lucky that Moonlight came along when he did," Rachel said.

"I'm off to Fairyland," Trixie said, nodding. "Let me send you back to your neighborhood, so you can trick-or-treat!" Trixie held up her wand, and a whirl of star-shaped fairy dust circled Rachel and Kirsty. The two girls waved to Trixie. The next thing they knew, they were back on Rachel's street.

The friends looked down the block to make sure no one had seen them. Then they grinned. "No more tricks for us tonight," Kirsty said.

Rachel nodded, holding up her candy bag and giggling. "Now I'm ready for some sweet treats!"

The Caramel
Apple Crisis

Contents

Ho-Hum Halloween

"Trick or treat!" Rachel and Kirsty said in chorus. They had been busy collecting candy since Trixie went back to Fairyland with the magic candy corn.

"We have lots of treats now," Kirsty said, looking in her pumpkin bag. "I'll have to save some chocolate for my mom. She always wants me to share with her."

Rachel laughed. "My dad loves candy, too. I got my sweet tooth from him," she admitted. Then she looked at her watch. "We can go to a few more houses before it's time to head to the town Halloween party."

Between ringing doorbells and greeting neighbors, Rachel and Kirsty stayed on the lookout for Trixie. They also watched for Moonlight, the clever kitten. After a few minutes, Rachel pulled out the invitation her parents had given her. There

was a picture of a spooky old house on the front.

"The party's at a new place," Rachel explained. "It used to always be on the other side of town, but my parents said we'd be able to walk this year. I'm pretty sure I know where this address is."

The girls walked along the sidewalk. As they got closer to the town party, there were clusters of kids and parents heading the same way. "This is it," Rachel announced, checking the street number on the invitation one more time. She stared down the long path to the old Victorian house.

"Really?" Kirsty questioned. "This is that spooky house we passed the other day. I thought you said no one lived here."

Overhearing the girls, a man dressed as a mad scientist stopped and raised his lab goggles. "This is the old Pratt mansion," he said. "The town bought it, and they're turning it into a community center."

"So this is where the new community center will be," Rachel said. "My parents were part of the planning group, but they kept the location a secret so they could surprise me."

"Well, this is the first event here," the man replied. "We'll see how it goes." As he waved good-bye and walked down the curvy path, Kirsty noticed he was wearing glow-in-the-dark rubber gloves and an old lab coat. Just then, the girls heard a family walk up behind them. "It's too scary," the little girl said to her father, who picked her up in his arms. "I don't want to go in there," she pleaded. The girl, dressed as a koala, buried her head in her father's shoulder and tried not to look.

Kirsty couldn't help agreeing with the little girl. "Even the trees are creepy," Kirsty said, noticing how the bare branches made long, fingerlike shadows. "It looks like that house has a lot of secrets."

"Not you, too!" Rachel giggled. "You'll feel a lot better once we find the magic caramel apple and bring back the Halloween spirit." She grabbed her friend's hand and pulled her down the path toward the old mansion.

Haunted House Party

Rachel and Kirsty gasped as they walked through the mansion door. "The decorations are fantastic," Kirsty murmured. Papier-mâché ghosts hovered in the air, and a giant spider web stretched from the floor to the ceiling. Bunches of orange and black balloons were tied to the grand staircase in the center of the first floor. Next to a stone fireplace, a rock band was playing "The Monster Mash." The musicians were all dressed as mummies, and music filled the house. A long table of food was right next to the grand staircase. Both girls noted that there were no caramel apples to be seen.

Before the friends could take it all in, Rachel's mom rushed up to them. "I'm so glad you two are here," she said. "We need people to start playing games and dancing. No one seems to be having fun."

Rachel looked around and realized that everyone was just standing around,

not talking or eating or laughing. She gave Kirsty a knowing look. No one would have any fun until the caramel apple was returned to Fairyland!

"We're happy to help, Mom," promised Rachel.

"Okay, how about you go to the third floor? That's where all the games are," Mrs. Walker said.

Kirsty looked up the tall staircase. It was like something out of an old movie.

"Let's start looking at the top and make our way down," she whispered to Rachel, who nodded. "The last piece of glitter candy might be

here." Judging from the glum faces on all of the party-goers, they needed to find the magic candy fast.

Once they climbed up to the third floor, the friends saw a long, skinny hallway. It was lined with bookshelves, and there were three dark wooden doors. A sign for a different activity hung on each door. "Let's go to the pumpkin-carving room first," Rachel suggested.

As soon as they stepped inside, they heard a group of boys bickering. "Your costume is silly," one of the boys said. "We were supposed to dress up as something *green*."

"So? I'm Peter Pan," the other boy said.

"Peter Pan isn't green," another responded. "He just *wears* green."

Rachel and Kirsty looked at each other with surprise. "They're goblins!" they whispered, realizing everyone in the group was wearing a green costume that

matched his skin. One goblin was dressed as a bunch of grapes, and another was a turtle. The two goblins pestering Peter Pan were dressed as trees.

All at once, a cloud of star-shaped fairy dust showered over Rachel and Kirsty. "Trixie!" they called, excited to see their friend, who quickly ducked behind Rachel's hair.

"Look, Trixie," said Kirsty, pointing. "Goblins. If they're here, the missing caramel apple must be nearby, too!"

"And they aren't alone," Trixie said softly. Then she motioned to a table in the corner where several kids had started carving pumpkins.

Rachel followed the fairy's gaze and gasped. There, sitting in the new Tippington Community Center, was Jack Frost!

Jack's Lantern

"*Brrr.* Just looking at him gives me chills," Kirsty confessed. There was something about Jack Frost's magic that made the air feel frigid whenever the troublemaker was around.

"I wonder what he's up to," Rachel said. "Let's find out."

The girls tiptoed closer and hid behind a stand-up skeleton. To their surprise, Jack Frost was carefully carving a mouth full of crooked teeth into his pumpkin. He leaned back and stared at the jack-o'-lantern. He seemed very pleased with himself.

All at once, Jack Frost looked up and glared around the room. He pushed his seat back and strode over to the gang of goblins. "What's going on here?" he inquired. "I thought I told you that we can't let the people have all the fun. Now get going and find that magic candy!"

"Well, that explains why he's here," said Kirsty.

"He wants to make sure they find the caramel apple," Trixie said thoughtfully. "Remember, just one bite from someone who doesn't believe in Halloween, and there won't be any Halloween spirit this year."

"Then we'd better hurry and find that apple first!" Rachel said. "My parents worked so hard on this center. I don't want the first party here to be ruined."

"What about your parents?" a voice said. The girls quickly turned around.

"Oh! Hi, Dad," Rachel gasped, brushing her hair forward to make sure Trixie was well hidden. "I just was telling Kirsty how much fun I'm having. You all did a great job planning the party."

"Well, thanks," Mr. Walker said, lifting his cowboy hat. "I wish everyone was having as much fun as you. Could you help in the next room for a minute? I need someone to run the game while I get more prizes."

"Sure thing," Kirsty said, hoping Rachel's dad wouldn't notice the goblins or Jack Frost.

As soon as Mr. Walker left, the friends rushed to the room where the Musical Chairs sign was posted.

The girls looked around. There were about ten kids sitting on chairs in the middle of the room. They all looked

bored. Most of the parents were
leaning against the wall.
"So, we need to start
and stop the music,"
said Rachel, heading
over to the CD
player.

"And take a chair
away each time,"
Kirsty said.

"And keep an eye
out for goblins!"
Trixie added.

"Okay. Is every-
one ready?" Rachel
called out, but only a
couple of kids nodded in
response. "Here goes.

Find a new seat when the music stops!" Rachel instructed. Then she pushed the PLAY button. As soon as the kids started to circle the empty seats, Jack Frost skipped into the room. He was holding his jack-o'-lantern, and it had a giant blue ribbon on it. "I won, I won," he sang, joining the kids who were playing musical chairs. Kirsty looked on, completely shocked. "I

guess I won't take a chair away," she said to Rachel, "since we have another player now." The best friends were used to trying to stay away from Jack Frost, but they couldn't exactly leave when they were in charge of the game!

Rachel nodded and pushed STOP. The kids all scrambled for a seat, and Jack Frost beat a ninja to the very last chair. He plopped his pumpkin in his lap and clapped his hands in joy. No one seemed to notice that Jack Frost was not a little kid. In fact, he was acting more like a kid than any of the children in the

room! The ninja
dragged his feet as he
headed over to his
father.

Just then, Rachel's
dad walked through the
door with a bag of
puzzles and whistles and
other prizes. "Thanks, girls," he said,
placing the bag next to the stereo on the
table. "You can go check out the other
rooms if you want."

At first, Rachel paused. She wondered
if they should stay there and keep an
eye on Jack Frost. Then a loud crash came
from the hallway, and she saw Moonlight
skitter past the open door. A crowd of
goblins, all in green, raced after him.

A Hidden Kitten

"Thanks, Dad," Rachel said, giving him a quick smile. Then she and Kirsty ran out the door and after the goblins. Almost immediately, the girls skidded to a stop. The goblins were huddled at the top of the staircase, each staring in a different direction.

"Where did that cat go?" the tallest goblin asked.

"It just disappeared," muttered one wearing a frog costume.

"It must be magic," guessed the Peter Pan goblin.

The goblins all looked confused, but

the goblin who was dressed as a bunch of grapes finally stamped his foot. "The cat could not have disappeared!" the goblin declared. "He just ran down the stairs before we could see him. Let's split up and find him. He showed up

whenever we found the other candies, so
he must know where the caramel apple
is, too!"

Kirsty and Rachel watched as the
goblins ran down the stairs and then
separated to search for the missing kitten.

Trixie peeked out from behind Rachel's
hair. "It's true," she whispered. "It seems
like Moonlight knew where to find the
other magic candy. Maybe he can help
us find the magic caramel apple."

"But first, we have
to find him before the
goblins do," Rachel
pointed out.

Suddenly, Trixie
raised a finger to her
mouth. "Did you
hear that?"

Rachel and Kirsty nodded. Then they heard it again . . . a tiny meow. "It sounds like it came from behind there," said Rachel, pointing to a bookshelf lining the hallway.

Kirsty examined the bookshelf on the wall. "Look!" exclaimed Kirsty. "Maybe it did!" One book appeared to be sticking out farther than the others. It was titled

The Secret Staircase. As soon as Kirsty pulled on the book's spine, the entire bookshelf slid to the side. There, sitting in the dark, was Moonlight. Behind him was a spiral staircase, almost impossible to see in the gloom.

"Meow, meow," the little cat said. He quickly turned around and disappeared down the mysterious staircase.

"He must want us to take this secret passageway," Trixie said. "Oh, what fun! Let's hurry."

Rachel and Kirsty looked at each other. It was one thing *finding* a hidden staircase, and another thing actually taking it. "I told you this house is full of secrets," Kirsty insisted.

"Come on!" Trixie said, flying into the dark stairwell. "How else will we save Halloween?" Trixie's wand started to glow, and the girls hurried after the fairy. The secret door slid shut behind them.

At once, the girls' wands began to glow as well. "I wonder how long it's been since someone was in here," Rachel mused, plucking a cobweb from her hair.

The wooden stairs
creaked with each
step she took

"I don't know,"
Trixie said, "but I
am sure Moonlight
has a special plan."

Kirsty hoped so.
She liked the idea of
a secret passageway, but this one was
spooky, dark and dirty, and the stairs
went in such a tight circle that she was
getting dizzy!

The three friends carefully descended
the gloomy staircase, looking for a hint
that would help them find the last piece
of glitter candy. But before they found any
clues, they reached the bottom of the stairs.

"Okay then," Kirsty said. "Let's look for a way out."

"This looks like it might work," Rachel commented, pointing to a doorknob with a fancy flower design on it. "I'll give it a try." She gave it a twist and a tug, and the door slid to the side just a crack. As a sliver of light entered the dark stairwell, Rachel peeked out. "It's the party room on the main floor! No one sees us! This must

be a secret door.
We're right near
the food table."

Trixie and
Kirsty rushed
over to have a
look. Trixie
hovered over
Rachel's head,
and Kirsty
ducked beneath.

"Yum!" said Kirsty. "I
see popcorn, pretzels, apple cider,
pumpkin muffins, and all kinds of candy.
But I still don't see —"

"I see caramel apples!" Trixie declared.

"Oh!" Rachel exclaimed. "They must
have just set them out. I see them, too.
And the one in the middle has a bright

orange glitter wrapper!"
Just as Rachel
said it, all three
friends gasped.
Someone was

standing by the apples and rubbing his
hands together gleefully. That someone
was Jack Frost!

A Festive Frost

"Oh no! He can't eat it!" Rachel yelled,
but Kirsty stopped her from opening the
door all the way.

"We need a plan," Kirsty explained.

"She's right," Trixie agreed. "If we go
out there now, Jack Frost will spot us,
grab the caramel apple, and we won't
have a chance."

Just then, a little boy dressed as a pirate walked up to the food table, right next to Jack Frost. Jack Frost stretched his bony fingers toward the magical caramel apple. "Shiver me timbers!" the young pirate bellowed suddenly, lifting up his eye patch for a better look. "I like your Jack Frost costume, matey. Did you make it yourself?"

The three friends hiding behind the door were surprised to see Jack Frost blush. "Um, well, my mother made it," he said.

Rachel and Kirsty looked at each other and giggled.

"It looks so real," the little boy said. "That's cool. I want to be Jack Frost next year."

"You make a good pirate," Jack Frost chuckled quietly. Then, without even looking, he reached out and grabbed the caramel apple with the glitter wrapper.

Trixie and the girls held their breath.

"Would you like this?" he asked the boy.

Rachel thought for sure that Jack Frost was teasing the little pirate, but his smile looked genuine. Just as the boy was about to take the apple, a goblin ran up and snatched it from his hands. "I got it!" the goblin shrieked.

"What? No! It was for him!" Jack Frost cried, but the goblin didn't seem to notice

that Jack Frost was even there. Just then,
another goblin snatched the caramel
apple away and held it up in the air.

"Hee, hee! Hooray for me!" the
goblin hooted. "I'm going
to give it to Jack Frost!"
Then he took off, holding
the apple in the air.

"What's happening?"
Rachel asked. "Don't
they know Jack
Frost is right here?"

"I guess not!" Trixie
laughed, shaking her head.

"We have to do something!"
Kirsty declared.

"Let's wait and see what happens,"
Trixie advised.

Just then, the Peter Pan goblin leaped up and clutched the caramel apple. "It's mine now!" he yelled, running across the room.

The parents at the party rolled their eyes, assuming the goblins were kids with horrible manners. The Peter Pan goblin cackled with joy as he ran, but he didn't watch where he was going. He tripped

over a witch's broom and went sprawling forward. The magic caramel apple flew from his hands and up toward the ceiling.

Suddenly, Trixie, Rachel, and Kirsty spotted Moonlight, perched on the chandelier. With a swat of his paw, Moonlight batted the caramel apple toward a bunch of balloons. The apple bounced right off! Everyone at the party

was trying to ignore the bratty goblins, so no one noticed the apple whiz over their heads and through a tiny open crack in the secret door.

"Wow! You caught it!" Rachel cried, gazing at Kirsty with excitement. "This time, the magic really did come to us!" she said with a laugh.

"Good catch!" Trixie exclaimed.

"Thank you so much." The Halloween fairy beamed as she tapped the apple with her wand and it shrank back to its Fairyland size. "I guess Moonlight had a plan all along. Now I need to hurry back to Fairyland,

so everyone can share in the magic of
Halloween! I'll be back soon."

As Trixie disappeared in a whirl
of fairy dust, Rachel and Kirsty
slipped out the secret door and joined
the party.

Rachel smiled. "I can't wait until
Trixie gets the last piece of candy back to
Fairyland."

"The party feels more fun already,"
Kirsty said, looking around. Then her
eyes stopped on an unusual sight. Kirsty
tugged on Rachel's sleeve and pointed.
Jack Frost was sitting in the corner with
his young pirate friend, and they were
both eating caramel apples.

"Hmm. Is it possible that he wasn't
after the magic caramel apple at all?"
Kirsty wondered.

Then she and her best friend looked each other in the eye. "No," they agreed, shaking their heads and giggling.

"And he's certainly not letting the people have all the fun. He's enjoying himself as much as anyone," Rachel admitted.

"Maybe Jack Frost just didn't want to be left out of the magic of Halloween," suggested Kirsty.

The band started back up, and the dance floor filled with ghosts and ghouls and goblins (some dressed as limes and lima beans). Rachel saw her parents laughing with Frankenstein and his bride.

Out of the corner of their eyes, the girls noticed a burst of glittery stars brighten the night sky. "Maybe it's Trixie," Kirsty said. The best friends rushed out the door and found Trixie sitting atop a round pumpkin.

"I wanted to come back and thank you," the fairy said. "And give you these pumpkin cookie jars from the king and queen. They are so grateful for all of your help. Now everyone can have a happy Halloween!"

"Thank you, Trixie. We had a lot of fun," said Rachel, lifting the lid off her cookie jar. It was filled with candy corn, chocolate bars, and caramel apples — all in orange glitter wrappers.

"This is so nice of you, Trixie," Kirsty added. "But are you sure that's the only reason you came back?"

At once, a little black cat bounded from the shadows. As Moonlight leaped toward Trixie, he magically shrank to his Fairyland size and landed in the fairy's lap. "Oh, Moonlight!" Trixie said with glee. "Now it is my happiest Halloween of all."

With that, the fairy and her kitten
vanished under a shower of stars.

"I guess it's time to join the Halloween
party," Rachel said, smiling at her friend.

"We should celebrate," Kirsty agreed.
"We got to help our friends, the fairies,
and there's nothing sweeter than that."

RAINBOW magic™

There's Magic in Every Series!

The Rainbow Fairies

The Weather Fairies

The Jewel Fairies

The Pet Fairies

The Fun Day Fairies

The Petal Fairies

The Dance Fairies

Read them all!

SCHOLASTIC

www.scholastic.com

www.rainbowmagiconline.com

SCHOLASTIC and associated
logos are trademarks and/or
registered trademarks of Scholastic Inc.
©2009 Rainbow Magic Limited.
HIT and the HIT Entertainment logo are
trademarks of HIT Entertainment Limited.

HiT entertainment

RMFAIRY

These activities are magical!

HIT and the HIT Entertainment logo are
trademarks of HIT Entertainment Limited.
© 2009 Rainbow Magic Limited.
SCHOLASTIC and associated logos are trademarks
and/or registered trademarks of Scholastic Inc.

📖 SCHOLASTIC
www.scholastic.com
www.rainbowmagiconline.com

HiT entertainment

RMACTIV

THE PETAL FAIRIES

Keep Fairyland in Bloom!

HIT and the HIT Entertainment logo are
trademarks of HIT Entertainment Limited.
© 2009 Rainbow Magic Limited.
SCHOLASTIC and associated logos are trademarks
and/or registered trademarks of Scholastic Inc.

■SCHOLASTIC
www.scholastic.com
www.rainbowmagiconline.com

HiT entertainment

PFAIRIES